This edition first published in Great Britain in 2000 by Mammoth
First published in Great Britain 1996 by Heinemann Young Books
imprints of Egmont Children's books Ltd, a division of Egmont Holding Ltd
239 Kensington High St, London W8 6SA
Published in hardback by Heinemann Library,
a division of Reed Educational and Professional Publishing Ltd,
by arrangement with Egmont Children's Books Ltd.
Text copyright © Helen Dunmore 1996
Illustrations copyright © Paul Dainton 2000
The author and illustrator have asserted their moral rights.
Paperback ISBN 0 7497 4228 3
Hardback ISBN 0 431 06182 3
10 9 8 7 6 5 4 3 2 1
A CIP catalogue record for this title is available from the British Library.
Printed in Dubai

Amina's Blanket

Helen Dunmore

Illustrated by Paul Dainton

YELLOW BANANAS

For my parents
P.D.

Chapter One

'JOSIE!' MISS HEATHER'S voice cracked across the classroom. Josie jumped.

'Dreaming again!' scolded Miss Heather. 'Well, you nearly missed something very exciting.'

But Josie couldn't believe that anything exciting was going to happen at ten o'clock on a wet Monday morning in Miss Heather's class.

'Right!' said Miss Heather. 'Wait two minutes and I'll bring it in.'

Then she went out with a mysterious smile, leaving the door open. What was she talking about? Josie stared across the table at Natasha.

5

'Blankets!' mouthed Natasha. If she talked out loud, Rosie Gold would tell on her.

'*Blankets?*' whispered Josie. 'What do you mean?'

But just at that moment Miss Heather swished
back into the classroom with a big, bulgy, black
plastic rubbish bag. She put it down on the table
next to Josie, and began to untie the string
round the neck of the bag. Rosie Gold pushed
forward to help her. The black bag wobbled on
the table as if there was something alive inside it.

Then the string was undone and
colour poured out like rain.
Red and gold and orange and
sparkling silver. Midnight
blue and kingfisher blue
and a white as fluffy as
a field of snow in the
sunlight. There was
forest green and warm,

buttery yellow and a rainbow ball like a patch of oil on the road after rain. The colours met and danced as they rolled out over the table.

'There!' said Miss Heather. 'Look what Mr Stassinopolous has given us for our blanket! Isn't it kind of him? Now, if each of you takes one ball of wool, and knits one square, we can sew them all up and make a beautiful warm blanket.'

Josie put up her hand. 'Please Miss, who's the blanket for?'

'Josie, you weren't listening at all, were you? Now, can someone tell her?'

Rosie Gold's hand wagged in the air, but for once Miss Heather did not choose her. She chose Jason Connolly.

'It's a blanket for someone who lives in a city where there's war. For an old person who hasn't got any heating.'

'Or a child,' chipped in Natasha.

'That's right, Jason,' said Miss Heather. 'Our blanket is going to go far away to the country I showed you on the map. It will go to help someone keep warm through the hard winter.

Lots of houses and flats have been damaged by shells because of the war. People are homeless.'

'Shells . . .' whispered Josie dreamily, thinking of the glisten of sea-shells on the sand when the tide went out. 'How can shells damage a house?'

'It's not that sort of shell. These shells explode, like bombs. They break walls and windows. They kill people,' said Natasha, who always listened when Miss Heather was talking.

'Oh,' said Josie. Then she put her hand up.

'Yes, Josie?' said Miss Heather.

'Is it snowing there, where the war is?' asked Josie.

'It snows there all winter long,' said Miss Heather, 'and often it's too dangerous for people to go out and gather wood to light fires. They get very cold.'

'Why don't they turn on the central heating then?' sniggered Darren Fox.

'They don't have central heating there, stupid!' Rosie Gold told him. Miss Heather looked sad.

'Oh yes, they do,' she said. 'They used to have nice flats with central heating, just like you, before the war. But the bombs and shells have destroyed them. Now, let's give these out. One ball of wool each.'

'I ought to have the gold,' said Rosie Gold, 'like my name, Miss.' Everyone wanted the gold, but Rosie got it. A crowd of hands snatched and pulled at the balls of wool. Then, suddenly, they were all gone except for a ball of dark blue that was a bit smaller than the others. Josie picked it up and squeezed its warm softness.

'It's not fair. Yours is the smallest,' said Natasha.

'I like it,' said Josie, and she did.

Miss Heather drew a square on the board and showed them how many stitches they had to do. They were allowed to take the wool home to do their knitting.

'I want this blanket finished by the end of the week!' said Miss Heather. 'Thirty beautiful squares.'

Chapter Two

AT HOME JOSIE knitted and knitted. Sometimes a hole came in her square and Mum had to help her pick up the stitches she had dropped. For a long time there was only a little wiggly strip of knitting on her needles, then suddenly her square started to grow.

'If I do six more rows tonight, it'll be finished,' she said to Mum on Wednesday. Her square looked like a little patch of midnight sky. Josie stroked it and wondered who would get the blanket. Would they like her blue square as much as she did?

That night Josie finished her square. She was not the only one. At school next morning the tables were covered with finished blanket squares. Red and gold and kingfisher blue and ebony black and green as bright as grass in summer. There was white like a corner of a snowy field, and a patch like the midnight sky. Miss Heather counted the squares.

'Thirty!' she said happily. 'Well done, Class Five. Now, all we've got to do is get the squares sewn up into a blanket.' She looked worried. 'But I don't know if I'll have the time to do it. There's a staff meeting this evening.'

Josie's hand shot up before anyone else's. 'My Mum'll do it!' she called out. 'She's really good at sewing.'

'Are you sure, Josie? Well, that would be a great help. If we fold all the squares and put them back in the sack, can you manage to carry it home?'

'Yes, of course,' said Josie.

Mum looked surprised when Josie tipped the bundle of squares onto the living room carpet. For a moment Josie thought she was going to be cross, but she wasn't.

'But you'll have to help, Josie. I can't do all this on my own,' she said.

First Mum ironed the squares, then they took thin wool and fat needles and started to sew them together. Josie sewed one strip of five squares, and Mum sewed another. Josie sewed

and sewed until her fingers were sore from
pushing the needle through the wool. All the
time she thought about the person in the cold
faraway city who would get the blanket. It was
very late and all the colours of the rainbow
were dancing in front of Josie's eyes.

'Thanks, Josie. You go to bed now. I'll finish
this,' said Mum.

When Josie was nearly asleep, Mum brought in the finished blanket. She spread it out on top of Josie's duvet. It was the most beautiful blanket in the world.

'Can I keep it here, just for tonight?' asked Josie.

'Yes, just for tonight,' said Mum.

Josie slept. Mum went to bed and the sky was as dark as the square of midnight blue Josie had knitted.

Chapter Three

A NOISE LIKE thunder woke Josie. She sat up and clutched the blanket. It felt warm and soft in her fingers, but the room had gone very cold. Josie shivered and pulled the blanket tight round her. The thunder rumbled again, and the room shook. Through the window Josie saw a patch of midnight sky, then a flash like lightning.

'Mum!' she whispered. She was too frightened to shout.

There was a rustling sound on the other side of the room, then a voice answered. But it wasn't Mum's voice. And the room didn't look like Josie's bedroom any more.

'Hello,' the voice said. 'Who are you?'

'Josie,' whispered Josie.

'Did the shells destroy your flat? Are you looking for shelter?' asked the voice. It sounded friendly. Josie peered round the room and saw a dark bundle on the floor, against the wall. She wrapped the blanket tight round her and tiptoed across to it. The floor felt like ice under her bare feet.

'You sound scared. You can stay here with me if you want, Josie,' said the voice.

Bright flashes like lightning lit the room. Josie saw that the bundle was a girl, curled up to keep warm. She was about the same age as Josie, and she had long dark hair, like Josie's.

Suddenly there was a terrible bang and the floor shook. Josie tripped up and fell onto the floor next to the girl.

'That shell came close,' said the girl. 'I hope it didn't hit any of my friends' flats. Oooh, what's that you've got? It's nice and warm and soft.'

'It's a blanket,' said Josie. 'You can put half of it over you if you want.' Josie wriggled close to the girl and spread the blanket over them both.

There was another bang and the wall trembled behind Josie's back.

'It's all right,' said the girl. 'That shell wasn't so close.'

'What's your name?' asked Josie.

'Amina.'

'Are you all on your own?'

'No,' said Amina. 'I've got a friend here. Give me your hand.' Amina took Josie's hand. 'Here, feel,' said Amina. Josie felt something soft and warm in Amina's hand. It was even softer than the blanket.

'Stroke him,' said Amina. 'He won't bite you.'

The something soft and warm was alive. It wriggled under Josie's fingers. 'What is it? A hamster?' asked Josie.

'No, he's my pet mouse. He used to be wild, but I tamed him. He's called Sinta. Only you mustn't tell, because food is so short and Mum won't let me give him anything.'

'Where's your Mum?'

'She went out to get wood, before it got dark,' said Amina. 'Only then they started shelling.

As soon as they stop, she'll come back. She always does.' But Josie felt Amina shivering. How cold and frightened she must be, lying alone on the floor all night, waiting for her mum to come home with wood to light a fire.

'You can have more of the blanket if you want. I'm not cold,' said Josie, and she tucked the blanket in round Amina.

'Poor little Sinta, I haven't got anything for you tonight,' said Amina. 'You'll have to wait till Mum gets back.'

'What does he eat?' asked Josie.

Amina laughed. 'The same as me!' she said. 'He hides in my pocket and has a little bit of whatever Mum brings back.' There was a soft squeak from Sinta.

'He knows we're talking about food,' said Amina. 'Where did you get this blanket, Josie? It must be the softest one in the city. It's even warmer than a fire.'

27

'You should see the colours!' said Josie. 'It's all made of squares of different colours. The one I knitted is dark blue, just the same colour as that patch of sky in the window.'

'I like it when the sky is dark blue, with no shell flashes,' said Amina. 'That means it's safe. Tell me more about the colours. Everything's so grey and dirty in the city now.'

'Well, there's a white like fluffy snow —' began Josie.

'Brrr, don't talk about snow! You'll make me feel cold again!'

'OK,' said Josie, and she tried to think of colours which would make Amina feel warm. 'There's yellow and red like the sun when it's going down on a holiday evening in summer. There's green like the shade of the trees when we sit under them in dinner hour. There's —'

Suddenly the window was full of a blinding white light.

A second later the room rocked. A crash like a thousand storms ripped through the building. It picked up Josie and Amina and threw them across the room. There was a terrible rumbling as if the building were falling apart, and the starlit sky showed where the window had once been. Josie's mouth was full of dust and smoke. She coughed and choked. The blanket was gone, Amina was gone, Sinta was gone. She could smell burning. How close was it? Was it in the building?

Chapter Four

'AMINA!' JOSIE WHISPERED. She couldn't shout because of all the dust.

'Josie!' came a little croaky voice from under the window.

'What happened? Did something hit us?'

'It was close. The closest we've had.'

'Is there a fire?'

The light in the window was changing to red. Amina got up and peered out. 'There's a fire just down the street,' she told Josie. Josie picked herself up off the floor and stumbled over to Amina. She saw long red flames licking out of a block of flats, and people, like black ants, running in the streets. Fire leapt into the sky, changing it from dark-blue to orange. It was nearly as light as day.

'Poor Sinta,' said Amina. 'He's so frightened of shells. He's afraid we'll get hit.'

'Where is he?'

'In my pocket, right down at the bottom. Can you feel him?' Josie felt the little shivering mouse, deep in Amina's pocket. The walls of Amina's room were shivering too.

'The fire is spreading,' said Amina. 'It's coming this way. I wish Mum was here.'

The fire crackled and rushed. It sounded as if it was nearly in the room. Then Josie and Amina heard voices shouting. The voices were coming nearer and nearer.

'Rescuers!' said Amina. 'They're coming to get us out!'

The fire was coming closer. Which would get to them first, the fire or the rescuers? Josie grabbed Amina's hand and they stumbled to the broken doorway. There was so much smoke that their eyes hurt. Josie coughed when she tried to breathe, and the fire roared like a lion outside. Suddenly the rescuers' voices were loud, just on the other side of the door.

'We're in here!' shouted Amina.

Chapter Five

THE DOOR FLEW open. Josie blinked as the bright sun chased across her bed. Mum was pulling back the curtains.

'Come on, Josie, you'll be late for school,' said Mum, 'and you've got to take that blanket in, remember.'

Josie felt on the bed for the blanket. It was there, as bright and beautiful as ever, all the colours of the rainbow.

'Amina!' whispered Josie. Where was Amina?

Josie picked up the blanket. It smelled of
smoke and danger. It smelled of war. Where
was Amina now?

Miss Heather packed the blanket up in a parcel and sent it away. Weeks passed. Everybody had forgotten about the blanket, except Josie. But one day Miss Heather came into the classroom waving a big brown envelope.

'Class Five!' she said. 'We've had a letter about our blanket. And some photographs.'

Miss Heather rustled in the envelope and held up a big photograph.

'Look,' she said. 'These are the people who have lost their homes because of the war. Their houses were shelled, and now they're in a centre for homeless people. If you look carefully, you can see the blankets on their beds. One of them is the blanket we made.'

The photograph showed a crowd of people huddled together in a big hall. There was a row of beds with blankets on them. And by one of the beds, there was a girl, about Josie's age, with long dark hair. Josie stared. Surely she knew that face. Josie could not stay in her chair. She had to get closer to the photograph.

'Josie!' said Miss Heather. But Josie was staring at the face of the dark-haired girl.

'Amina!' she whispered. 'It's Amina! The girl in my dream!'

It *was* Amina in the photograph. And one hand was in her pocket. Josie knew she was stroking Sinta.

'Sit down, Josie!' said Miss Heather crossly, and Josie had to sit down.

'Our blanket is on one of those beds,' said
Miss Heather.

But Josie knew it was on Amina's bed.
Amina isn't a dream, she thought, *she's
a real girl. My dream was real.
Amina had to leave her
home because of the
shelling and the fire.*

The blanket was on Amina's bed in the centre for homeless people. All the colours of the rainbow were there. The red, the gold, the orange, the forest green, the snowy white and the midnight blue that Josie had knitted. The blanket would wrap round Amina at night and keep her warm.

'Sleep well, Amina,' said Josie, so softly that no one heard her.

Yellow Bananas are brilliantly imaginative
stories written by some of today's top writers.
These beautifully illustrated books provide
an excellent introduction to chapter books.

**So if you've enjoyed this story, why
not pick another from the bunch?**